History's Mysteries

King Tut

Is His Tomb Really Cursed?

Megan Cooley Peterson

Bolt is published by Black Rabbit Books
P.O. Box 227, Mankato, Minnesota, 56002.
www.blackrabbitbooks.com

Jennifer Besel, editor; Grant Gould, designer;
Omay Ayres, photo researcher

Cataloging-in-Publication Data is available at the Library of Congress.
ISBN 978-1-68072-411-0 (hardcover)
ISBN 978-1-64466-258-8 (paperback)
ISBN 978-1-68072-527-8 (ebook)

Image Credits

Alamy: KGPA Ltd, 18; robertharding, 24 (b); Steve_Davey, 16–17 (sarcophagus); annubismumblings.tumblr.com: forceyourway, 23 (l); chuchotezvous.ru/: Teammy, 22 (r); commons.wikimedia.org: Jschultz1129, 6, 24 (t); Flickr.com, dalbera/Flickr, 14, 15 (both); Dreamstime: Neil Harrison, 12 (bkgd); egykingblog.com: Egypt King, 22 (l); Getty: Dorling Kindersley, 23 (r); GraphicaArtis, 4–5; indiatimes.com: juharizsuzsanna, 21; iStock: rysp, 1; Shutterstock: babysofja, 8–9 (amulet); Catmando, 10–11; doom.ko, 29 (mask); dovla982, 12–13 (map); Jaroslav Moravcik, Cover (mask), 3, 8–9 (mask), 26–27; Maria Isaeva, Cover, 29 (magnifying glass); mountainpix, 32; Naeblys, 16–17 (tomb); Netfalls Remy Musser, 31; Oleg Golovnev, 29 (paper)
Every effort has been made to contact copyright holders for material reproduced in this book. Any omissions will be rectified in subsequent printings if notice is given to the publisher.

CONTENTS

CHAPTER 1

DISCOVERY in the Desert

It was February 1923. Howard Carter was about to make history. He stood outside King Tutankhamen's burial chamber. He had explored the rest of the tomb. Now he hoped to find the king's mummy.

Some stories say Carter hid a tablet found in the tomb. The tablet said death would come to those who **disturbed** the king.

A Legendary Curse

Some people believed Tut's tomb was **cursed**. Carter and his team broke through the sealed door anyway. Inside lay Tut's mummy. It had not been touched for more than 3,000 years.

After the discovery, people close to the team died. Was Tut's tomb really cursed?

THE CURSE OF KING TUT

Several people connected to Tut's tomb got sick or died.

February 16, 1923
Carter and his team open the burial chamber.

April 5, 1923
Lord Carnarvon dies. Carnarvon paid for the search of Tut's tomb. His dog dies the same day.

July 10, 1923
Prince Ali Kamel Fahmy Bey is murdered after visiting the tomb.

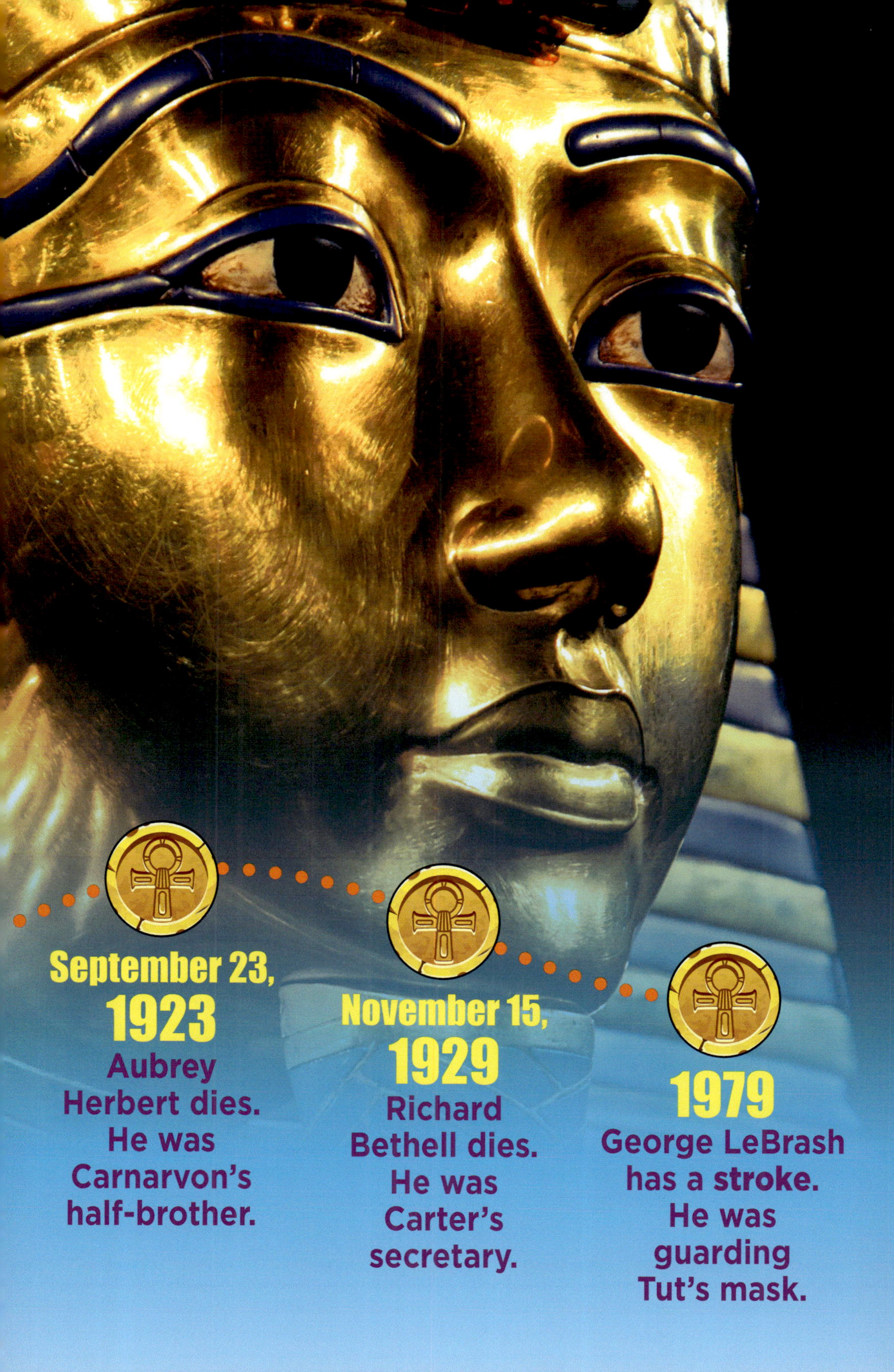
September 23,
1923
Aubrey
Herbert dies.
He was
Carnarvon's
half-brother.
November 15,
1929
Richard
Bethell dies.
He was
Carter's
secretary.
1979
George LeBrash
has a **stroke**.
He was
guarding
Tut's mask.

CHAPTER 2

HISTORY of King Tut

King Tut ruled Egypt from about 1333 to 1323 BC. He became **pharaoh** around age nine. He died about 10 years later. His time as king was uneventful. Tut became famous only after Carter found his tomb.

Africa

Valley of the Kings

The Valley of the Kings is an area in Egypt. Many royal tombs were cut into the rock there. Robbers broke into many of the tombs. They stole the treasures inside. So far, Tut's is the most **intact** royal tomb ever found.

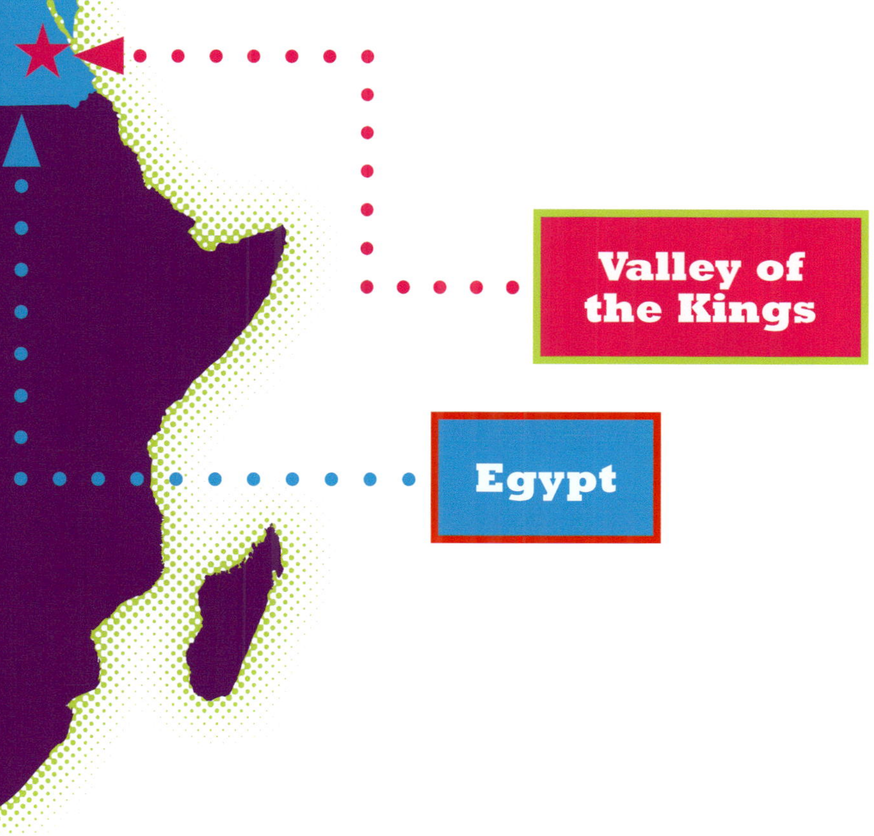

Objects for the Afterlife

Carter found thousands of objects in Tut's tomb. Ancient Egyptians believed Tut needed them in the **afterlife**. The objects included model boats and jewelry.

Treasures in the Tomb

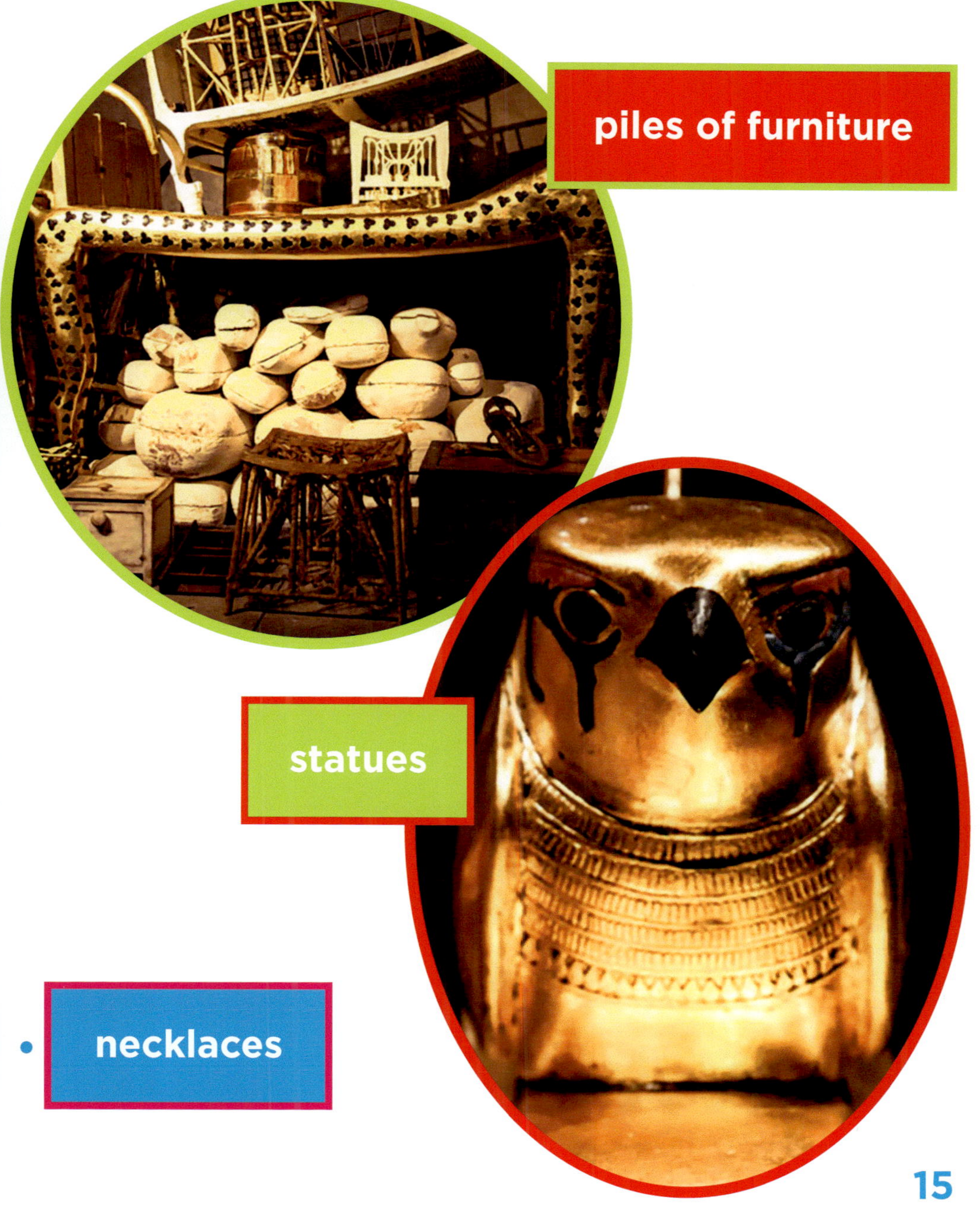

piles of furniture

statues

necklaces

INSIDE TUT'S TOMB

burial chamber

room had Tut's throne, chariots, and about 700 other objects

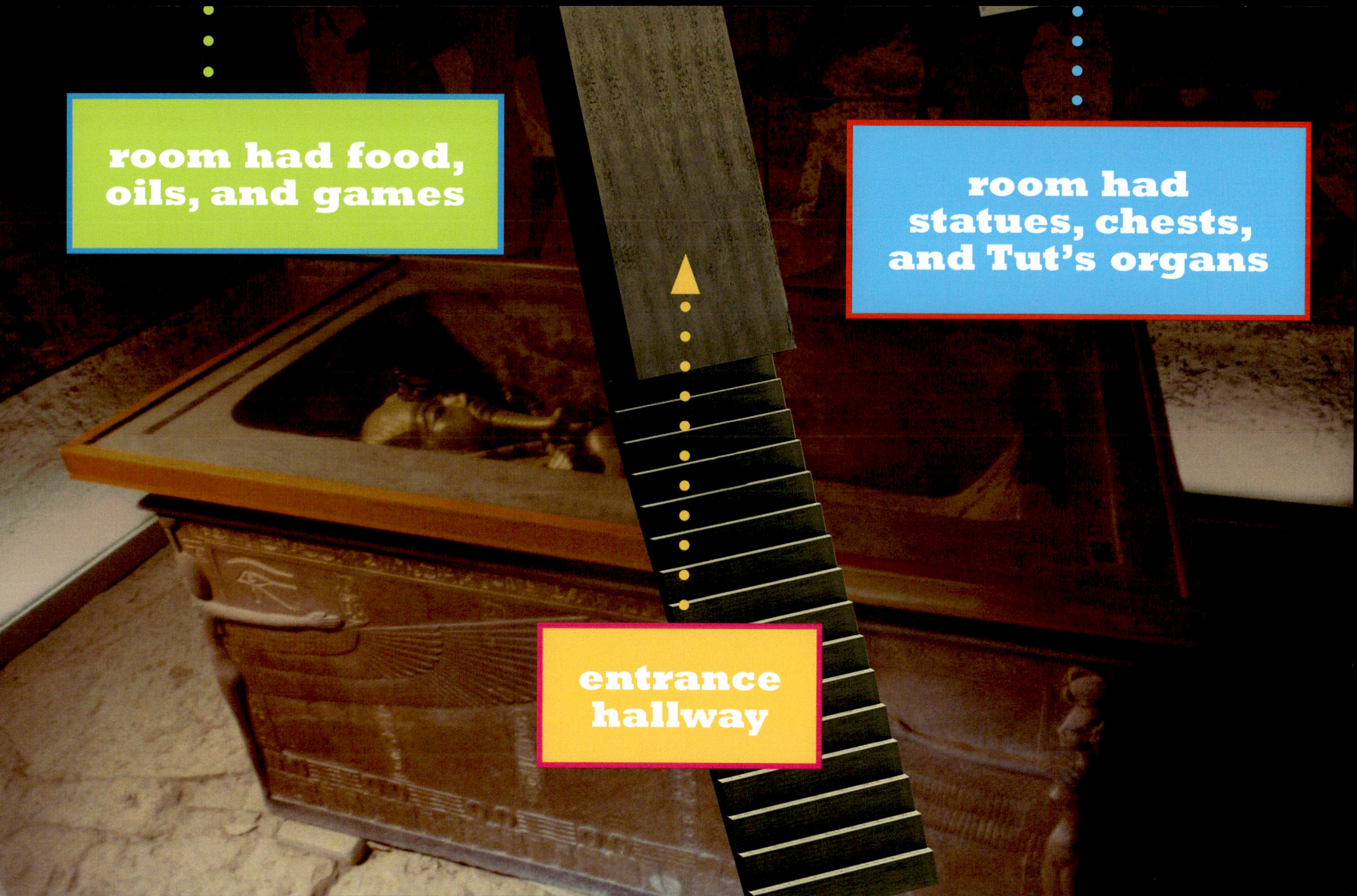
room had food, oils, and games
room had statues, chests, and Tut's organs
entrance hallway

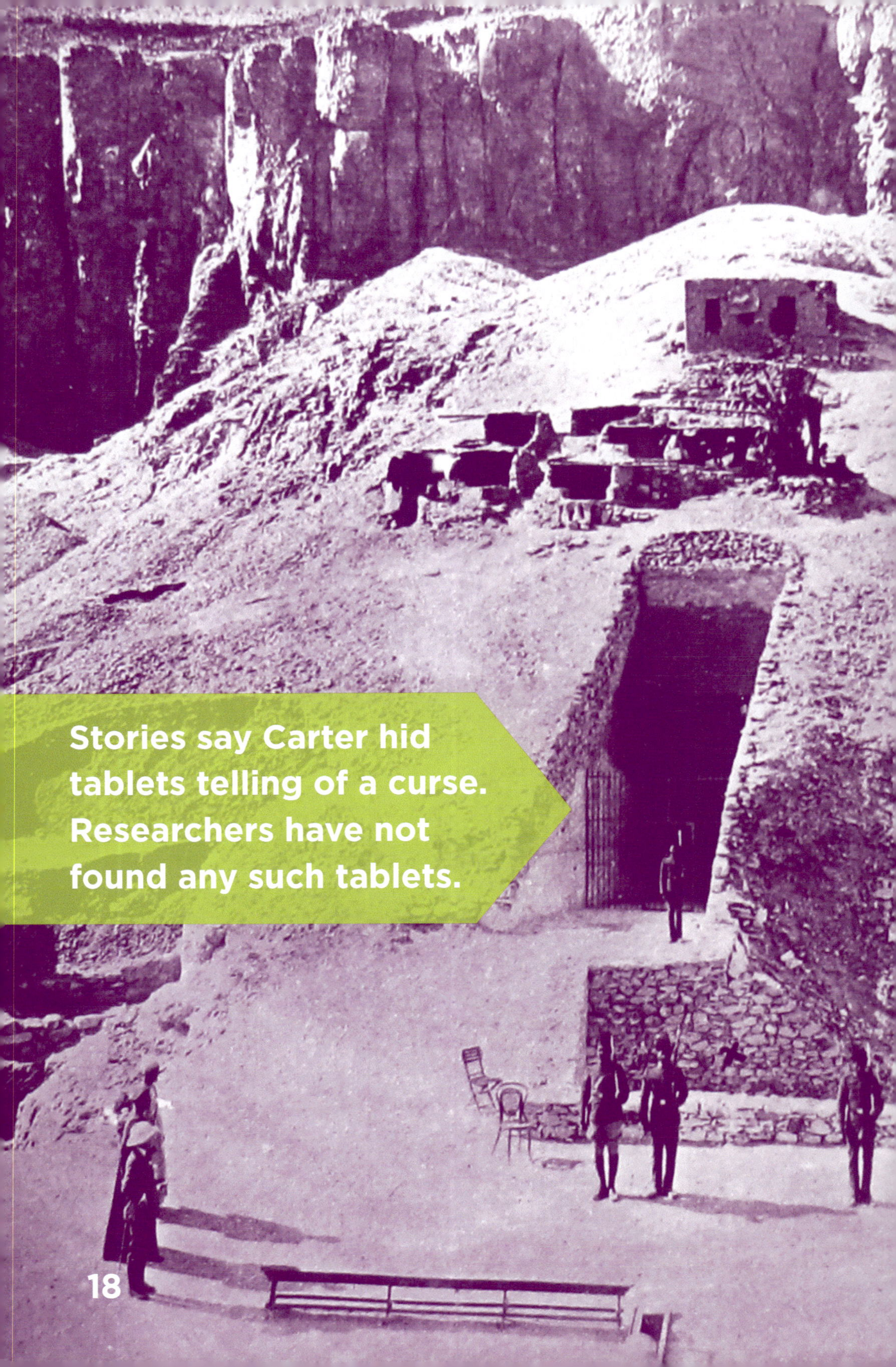

Stories say Carter hid tablets telling of a curse. Researchers have not found any such tablets.

CHAPTER 3

INVESTIGATING the Mystery

Historians have studied Tut's mummy. They all have the same questions. How did the young king die? Is there any truth to the curse?

Some people say Carter made up the curse. He didn't want anyone else to disturb the tomb.

A Possible Murder

A man named Ay helped the young king rule. He became king after Tut's death. An X-ray of Tut's skull showed bone pieces in the skull. Something might have hit Tut's head. Did Ay kill Tut to become king?

Recent scans of Tut's skull tell a different story. Scientists found no skull **fractures**. They say the bone pieces came loose after Tut died.

Some people believe Tut's murder caused a curse.

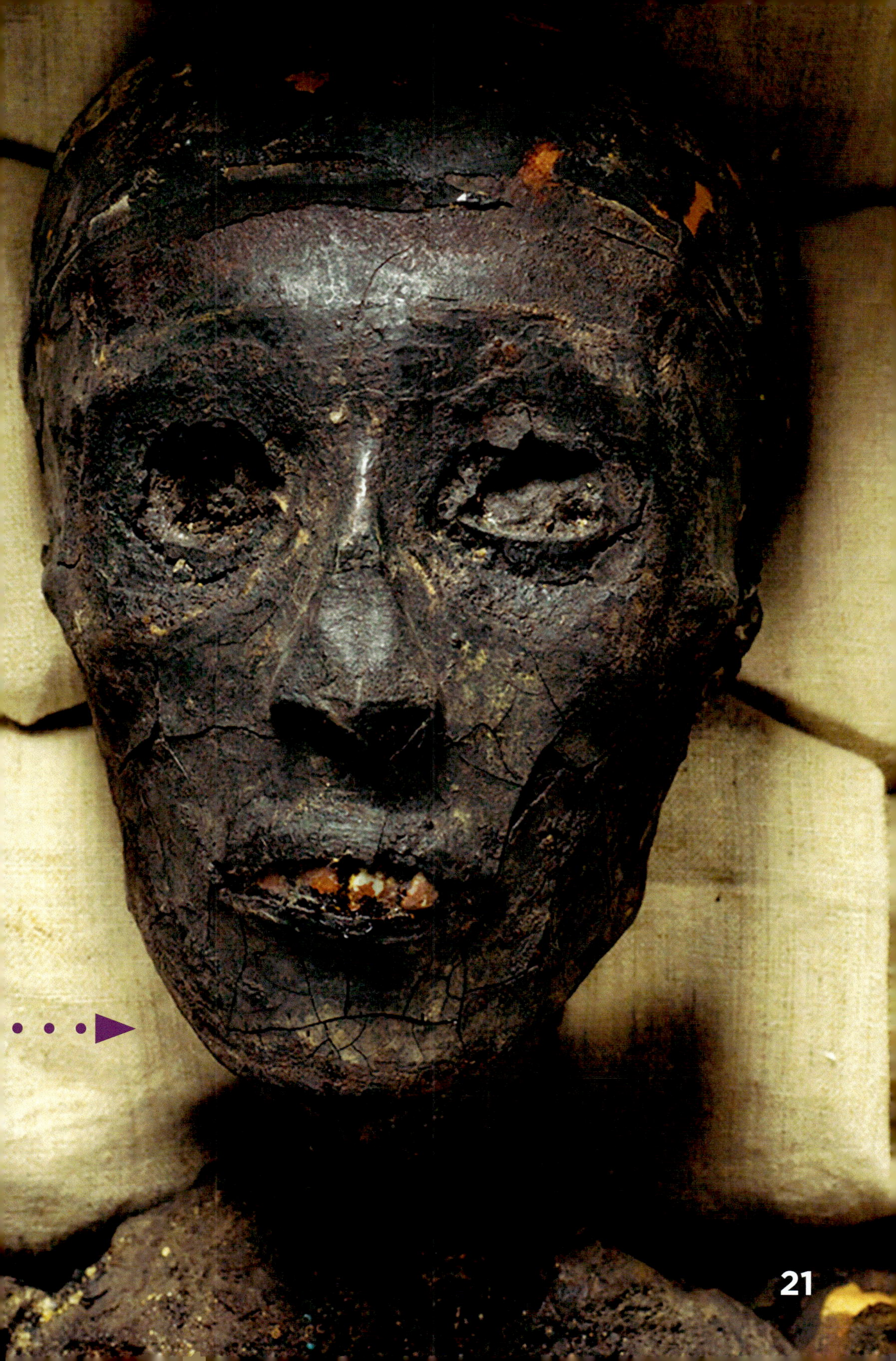

HOW TO MAKE AN EGYPTIAN MUMMY

Scientists can study Tut's body because it was well preserved.

Remove organs. Cover body in salt for 40 days.

Step 1

Stuff body with linen, straw, or sawdust.

Step 2

Wrap body in fabric and resin.

Step 3

Place mummy inside a coffin.

Step 4

Carter and his team damaged Tut's mummy. To remove it from the coffin, they cut the body into 18 pieces.

A Broken Leg

Another theory is that Tut died from **infection**. His left thigh bone was broken. Researchers found resin in the break. They say this shows Tut broke his leg before he died. An infected leg could have killed him.

CHAPTER 4

You Decide

King Tut died more than 3,000 years ago. Does a curse hang over his tomb? The mystery lives on.

Asking Questions to Solve the Mystery

Researchers ask questions to solve history's mysteries. You can too!

Who worked with Carter?

What makes this story interesting?

When did stories about a curse start?

Where was the curse story reported?

WHY?

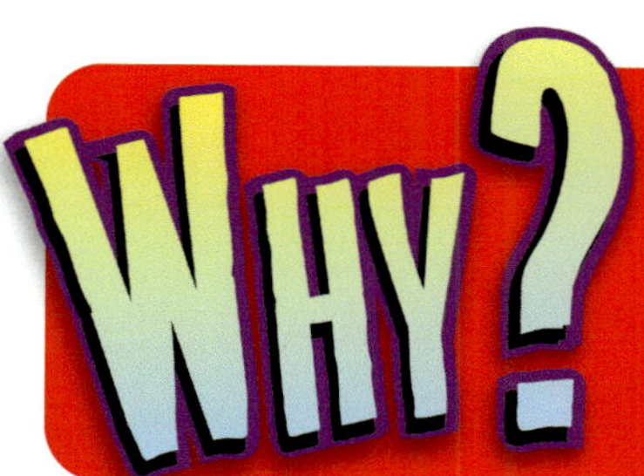

Why do some people think Carter hid tablets?

HOW?

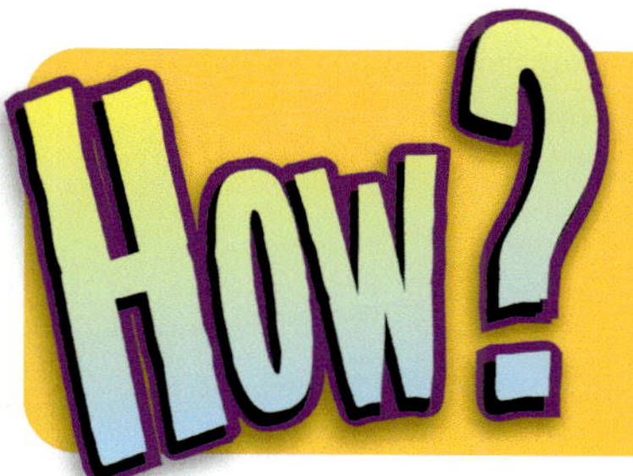

How did ancient Egyptians learn to make mummies?

What other questions do you have?

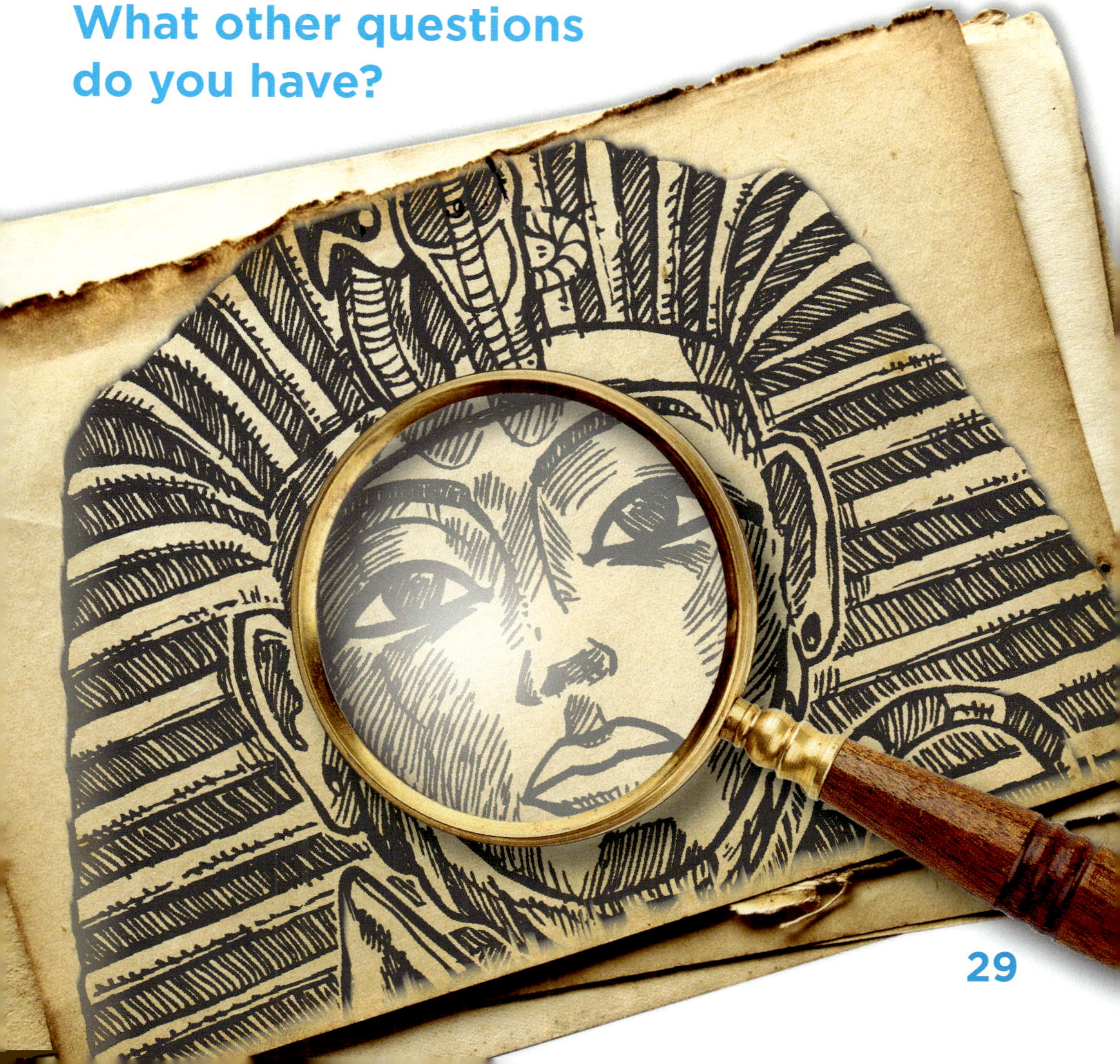

afterlife (AHF-tur-liyf)—a life after death

cursed (KURSD)—to be under an evil spell meant to cause harm

disturb (di-STURB)—to bother or change in some way

fracture (FRAK-chur)—a break in hard tissue, such as bone

infection (in-FEK-shun)—a disease caused by germs that enter the body

intact (in-TAKT)—untouched especially by anything that harms it

pharaoh (FAYR-oh)—a ruler of ancient Egypt

preserve (pree-ZURV)—to keep alive, intact, or free from decay

resin (REH-zen)—a yellowish or brownish substance from the sap of some trees

stroke (STROK)—a serious illness caused by a blocked or broken blood vessel in the brain

BOOKS

Owen, Ruth. *King Tut: The Hidden Tomb.* Egypt's Ancient Secrets. New York: Bearport Publishing, 2017.

Ridley, Sarah. *Life in Ancient Egypt.* Everyday History. Mankato, MN: Smart Apple Media, 2016.

Stewart, David. *You Wouldn't Want to Be Tutankhamen!: A Mummy Who Really Got Meddled With.* You Wouldn't Want to Be ... New York: Franklin Watts, an Imprint of Scholastic Inc., 2017.

WEBSITES

10 Facts about Ancient Egypt!
www.natgeokids.com/uk/discover/history/egypt/ten-facts-about-ancient-egypt/

The Curse of King Tut's Tomb
www.youtube.com/watch?v=6Xv8dCIWi6w

Tutankhamun Facts!
www.natgeokids.com/uk/discover/history/egypt/tutankhamun-facts/

INDEX